" Then I look over at Ethan. His grey eyes are peering between long greasy strands of bedraggled fair hair.

He's a bit of a crawler with teachers and he tries to attach himself like a limpet to boys in our class, but he's about as popular as a skunk. "

Magpie
by Jill Atkins

Published by Ransom Publishing Ltd.
Unit 7, Brocklands Farm, West Meon, Hampshire
GU32 1JN, UK
www.ransom.co.uk

ISBN   978 178591 143 9
First published in 2016

BREAKOUTS

MAGPIE

Jill Atkins

Ransom

ONE

Nobody speaks to me. I sometimes believe they think, if they notice me at all, that I'm just boring old Grace, the non-person. I sit like a quiet brown mouse in my corner of the class and watch.

Ethan, Megan, Sandeep, Scarlett, Kyle and the rest are crowded round Jassy like fluttering moths round a hypnotic candle. She's rather like a candle, Jassy. Tall and slender with flowing blonde hair that flickers with iridescent lights as she tosses her head in laughter. No wonder they admire her. I do, too. But I'm not into hero-worship like they are.

But would I love to be in her shoes: popular, rich and attractive, as she is? You bet I would!

'OK, everyone,' she calls, serious in class prefect mode for a moment. 'Sorry to be a pain, but you know Ms Joseph left me in charge. We're supposed to be revising, don't forget.' Most of them return to their places and open their books. I watch them pretend to read, learn facts, but eyes stray in her direction, hoping she will give them a smile or an encouraging nod.

Ms Joseph, our form teacher, has only left us for ten minutes. She'll be back soon. Besides, I want to pass my exams, so I try to concentrate on the words on the page. History! If only I could memorise the facts, but they pass through my eyes and out the back of my head.

'My watch!'

I'm torn away from the past and jolted back to the present. Sandeep is standing up at his desk. He is frantically waving his left arm and his patka is bouncing up and down in his agitation.

'My watch! It's gone!'

'Well, it wasn't me!' Kyle shouts his denial, standing with his legs wide apart and his hands on his knees, like a sumo wrestler. Megan leaps up, laughing loudly and whirling in a dance, like a dervish. Everyone ignores her. Jassy hurries over to Sandeep and inspects his bare wrist.

'What's it like?' she asks.

'Black dial and strap … it's my new sport watch … waterproof … shockproof … stopwatch … '

A few people bend down to search the floor.

'When did you last have it?' Jassy coos.

'Er, not sure,' says Sandeep, scratching his ear. 'I know I was wearing it when I left home, because I checked the time when my bus didn't come.'

'Oh, poor you, Sandeep,' she says. 'I hope it turns up soon.' With a sympathetic smile, she returns to her desk.

I look around at the class. Most people have forgotten all about the watch already. Kyle is still denying being the thief, although no one has actually accused him. Megan's eyes are wild and she's sitting on her desk facing the back of the room.

Then I look over at Ethan. His grey eyes are peering between long greasy strands of bedraggled fair hair. He's a bit of a crawler with teachers and he tries to attach himself like a limpet to boys in our class, but he's about as popular as a skunk. Only the other day I saw him pestering Sandeep and I heard Sandeep explode.

'Clear off, Ethan!' he shouted. 'You're worse than a leech trying to suck my blood!'

After a moment, Ethan begins studying his book rather too studiously. Does he know something about the watch? Could he have taken it to repay Sandeep for the way he and the other boys in the class treat him?

Getting out the little notebook I always carry around with me, I begin to jot down what I think.

*

With a click of high-heeled shoes and the swish of her full skirt, Ms Joseph breezes in. She looks at Jassy, eyebrows arched in question.

'I heard raised voices. What's going on?' she demands. 'I expected to find all heads down … '

'Oh, it's nothing really, Ms Joseph.' Jassy beams her brightest sunny smile. 'Sandeep has mislaid his watch.'

Ms Joseph nods and turns to Sandeep who is still standing, a deep frown on his face.

'Not to worry, Miss,' he mutters. 'I must have dropped it. I'll look for it at break.'

I keep one eye on Ethan while I try to study. He's got a sneaky smile in the corner of his mouth. Definitely suspect! Or could Kyle or Megan – or someone else in the class be guilty? I aim to find out.

TWO

Sandeep's watch doesn't turn up at break and I'm curious about Ethan, so I follow him around. He's alone, like me, and he's not trying to win friends, for once.

At lunchtime, I touch Jassy's hand as she passes my desk.

'Sandeep's watch,' I whisper. 'I think I might know who took it.'

'Yeah?'

'Yeah … well, I've got three main suspects so far.'

She smiles. 'Quite the detective! Who?'

'Ethan … or maybe Megan … or Kyle.'

'What makes you suspect them?' she asks.

I begin to tell her, but then Scarlett and some other girls gather round, fluttering and fussing around Jassy's brightness. I'll have to tell her my reasons when I get the chance. As long as I can speak to her alone, I know she'll listen. She would never think of me as a friend, but she's always been kind to me. That's what I like about her.

As soon as the bell goes at the end of the afternoon, Jassy slips out of class. I try to catch her up, but when I get outside she's gone. I wonder if she is meeting someone. Maybe she has a secret boyfriend!

As I give up trying to catch Jassy, I notice Ethan prowling at the corner of the school building. A few moments later, I see Sandeep and two of his mates strolling towards him. I duck behind a litter bin. It stinks like someone's left a dead rat in there, but it keeps me well hidden. I peer out.

'I'm sorry about your watch, Sandeep,' Ethan says.

Sandeep stops.

'You can borrow mine if you like,' Ethan goes on, beginning to undo his watch strap. 'I've got a spare one at home.'

Sandeep smiles and I'm waiting for the sarcastic remark from him or his friends.

'Thanks, but no thanks,' Sandeep says.

I gasp and almost reveal my hiding place. Sandeep being polite to Ethan? That's a first! The boys wander off home, leaving Ethan looking as surprised as I am. That was kind of him to offer his watch. Surely, a thief wouldn't have done that? Maybe he's not as obnoxious as I thought.

We're in registration the following morning when the next incident occurs.

'Has anyone seen my silver ring?' Scarlett calls. She's got tears in her eyes and her face matches her name. 'It's a special one my Dad gave me last birthday.'

It's a very pretty ring. I remember admiring it a few days ago. We're not allowed to wear jewellery at school, but she kept it in a glittery little drawstring bag.

Most people shake their heads and look around at each other, trying to work out who is the culprit.

'What would I want with a silver ring?' Kyle asks. 'That's for girls!'

Megan rolls her eyes and shakes her head violently, waving her right hand provocatively. She's wearing a silver ring. Trust her to break the school rules! Is it Scarlett's? Scarlett approaches her and peers at the ring, then shakes her head. It's not hers.

Jassy puts her arm around Scarlett. 'We'll all help you hunt for it,' she says. 'It would be a shame for you to lose it. I know you love pretty things. I do, too.'

By pure accident, as I pull out my notebook, I catch Ethan's eye. I look away sharpish, but when I glance up again he's still staring at me. I feel a blush spread over my face and neck. Why is he gawping at me?

I've forgotten all about him by the end of the afternoon. I've missed the chance to talk to Jassy again and I'm walking slowly out of school when he leaps out at me. My heart beats like a djembe.

'I saw you ducking behind that bin yesterday, Grace!' His face is only centimetres from mine. 'Were you spying on me?'

'No!' I back off.

'You were! I'm not stupid, you know. Ever since Sandeep's watch went missing, you've been staring at me. You reckon it was me who took it, don't you?'

'No!'

'Don't lie! I see you sitting there all innocence, but I know you're watching all the while; writing in that little notebook of yours.'

This time I don't reply. It's true, what he says.

'Admit it!'

I sigh. 'All right, I did wonder if it was you. I thought you looked suspicious. You had an odd smile on your face, as if you knew something about it. And I overheard what Sandeep called you the other day, so I thought you might be getting your own back, but … '

'But what?'

I hesitate. Should I delete him from my suspect list so easily?

'Come on, Grace, tell me.'

'Oh … all right … I … I don't think so now.'

'So what changed your mind?'

'You offered to lend Sandeep your watch. I don't think you'd have done that if you'd stolen his.'

Ethan flicks his hair away from his face and grins. 'You're a bit of a detective in your quiet way. How come?'

I shrug my shoulders. 'Well, I read lots of detective novels, and … '

'Hey! So do I.' He chuckles. 'I quite fancy myself as a famous detective.'

I haven't seen his face look so cheerful before and I smile. At that moment, a brainwave strikes like a flash of electric current in my head. 'Ethan,' I say, hoping I'm not being too impetuous. 'D'you fancy working together? Maybe we'll be able to find out who took Sandeep's watch and Scarlett's ring.'

Ethan holds out his hand and we shake. 'A deal,' he says. 'We'll begin tomorrow.'

THREE

I hadn't realised that Ethan lives near me, but he's on my bus in the morning. He's washed his hair and it's gelled back off his face. A definite improvement! We walk towards school together. It feels strange after being on my own for so long.

'So, apart from me,' he asks, as soon as we've leapt off the bus, 'who are your chief suspects?'

I look at him out of the corners of my eyes. I think I

might like having him as a companion. He's not quite such a creep as I first thought, but I'm not absolutely sure I can trust him yet. Has he forgiven me for suspecting him?

'Tell me yours first,' I say.

'OK, I think it might have been Kyle.'

I jump ahead like an excited March hare and stand in front of him, so he has to stop abruptly.

'Me, too,' I say. 'But why?'

'Well, his dad's been out of work forever and his family is really poor. His toes are bursting out of the holes in his shoes … '

'I know,' I say. 'His clothes are really old – and they live in that dreadful ruin of a house. I can't help feeling sorry for him. He never has anything new or money for school trips, but … '

' … and Sandeep's watch is a really good one. Worth quite a bit. Tempting … '

I nod. 'And Scarlett's ring is real silver … '

'I don't like the way Kyle denied being the thief so loudly both times. My grandad says that could be a sign of guilt. That's what convinced me.'

We start walking again. 'OK,' I say after a while. 'Anyone else?'

'Your turn,' he says.

'Megan.'

'Why her?'

'She's weird,' I say. 'Always showing off. She's been in trouble before. I don't know what she did, but it must have been serious, or why does she have a social worker?'

We walk in silence until we're a hundred metres from school. 'We'd better go in separately,' I whisper. 'People might get the wrong idea!'

Ethan's chuckle is infectious and I have to join in,

but we both swipe the laughter from our faces as we almost bump into Kyle. He looks dishevelled, as if he has just rolled out of a haystack and his coat is as tatty as a scarecrow's. He certainly has a motive for stealing.

'Eyes and ears open!' whispers Ethan, as we split up.

'Yeah. See you later.'

First lesson is science, learning about combustion. I keep away from Ethan. I know he is watching everyone as avidly as I am, but I don't notice anything unusual as we all do some experiments using Bunsen burners. My favourite is burning magnesium to make flares as blinding as the winter sun shining on snow.

I'm busy drawing the Bunsen burner and wondering how I can show such a dazzling white in my diagram when there is a scream. Megan has picked up the flaming burner, pointing it at another girl and singeing her hair.

'Get out!' screams Mrs Davey. 'Go straight to Mrs Metcalf!'

We all know what that means. Our headteacher is as fierce as a fire-breathing monster and her flames are as hot as the Bunsen burner. No one escapes her clutches without being badly burned. Megan grabs her school bag and stomps out, yelling abuse at Mrs Davey. That's not the first time Megan has acted dangerously in the science lab. She could be expelled for doing that.

✳

Megan isn't in the last lesson with Ms Joseph.

'I have something very serious to say to you all,' says Ms Joseph.

I think it's going to be about Megan, but it isn't.

'I've had a very worrying conversation with Mrs Davey,' she says. 'Since your science lesson this morning, she has discovered that several items of equipment have gone missing from the laboratory. Do any of you know anything about this?'

We all shake our heads.

'Jassy?'

Jassy jumps as if a fire cracker has gone off behind her. Her hair flickers like a candle flame in the wind.

'Yes, Ms Joseph?'

'You'll let me know if you see or hear anything suspicious, won't you?'

'Oh, yes, of course. Did Mrs Davey tell you what's missing?'

'Yes. A pair of metal tongs, a test tube holder and an electronic balance.'

When Ms Joseph lets us go, I catch up with Ethan.

'Do you think Megan took those things?' I whisper. 'Her bag looked really heavy when she stormed out of the lab.'

'Good thinking!' Ethan grins. 'It's Grace on the case!'

＊

I'm surprised Megan is allowed back in school the next day, but I expect her social worker must have put out some of Mrs Metcalf's fire.

The thefts continue. First, Sally's sparkly pencil case then Edward's cricket ball. I make copious notes in my book, and Ethan and I keep watch, but neither of us witnesses anything suspicious. The thief is too clever for us.

In our art lesson that afternoon, Megan is in trouble again. She paints her face green and claims she is the Incredible Hulk. The whole class stops work to stare at her, and several people laugh. Mr James sends her out of the lesson. I can't understand why she has to behave so badly.

At the end of the day, Ms Joseph stands up as stiff as a gate post.

'I'm shocked to hear there has been a theft from the art room,' she says. 'And you are all implicated as it must have happened during your lesson.'

'It was probably Megan,' says Ethan.

Ms Joseph ignores him and continues. 'This is getting quite out of hand. Mrs Metcalf is deciding whether to call in the police, but before that I've promised to investigate for myself. Before you go home, I want to you all to empty the contents of your bags onto your desks.'

Someone mutters something about infringement of human rights, but I just sigh and empty my bag. Then my mouth drops open.

'Grace?' Glowering like a storm cloud, Ms Joseph hovers over me, pointing at a set of fine paint brushes among the debris on my desk. 'What is the meaning of this?'

FOUR

My blood pounds in my head like the beat of a rock band.

'I didn't take them, Ms Joseph. Honestly, I didn't.'

'So how did they miraculously appear in your bag? By osmosis?'

I'm shaking so uncontrollably I have to sit down. I'm supposed to be the one investigating this, not the accused. 'I don't know.' I feel tears pricking my eyes.

'It wasn't Grace.' Ethan steps forward. 'I was next to her the whole time in art.'

'I was close to her, too,' says Jassy.

'So someone must have planted them in her bag,' says Ethan.

Ms Joseph's stormy expression darkens. 'Grace, did you leave your bag at all while you were in art?' she asks.

'No, Ms Joseph, I don't think so.'

In contrast, Ethan's face brightens and I can almost see the cogs working inside his brain.

'It must have happened when Megan got thrown out. We were all watching her. Anyone could have done it then.'

Ten minutes later, we all head for the door. I've been 'let off with a caution', as Ms Joseph put it. As soon as

I'm clear of the school gates, I hear clomping footsteps catching up with me.

'So who did put those brushes in your bag?' It's Ethan.

I shrug my shoulders. The subject is too raw in my mind to want to discuss it.

'Come on, Grace. You're the detective, remember? You know and I know you didn't pinch them. So let's go from there.'

'OK.'

It's really strange, two solitary people, me and him, becoming friends so suddenly, after ignoring each other for years, but I feel so comfortable with him, like we've been friends for ages.

We sit on a bench at the edge of the shopping centre and I take out my notebook. I list everything under the headings:

Items stolen:	From:	Suspects:
watch	Sandeep	Kyle
ring	Scarlett	Megan
pencil case	Sally	????
cricket ball	Edward	
metal tongs, test tube holder, electronic balance	science lab	
paint brushes	art room	

It's therapeutic writing it all down, but it doesn't solve the mystery.

We walk the rest of the way home.

'I wonder what will be stolen tomorrow,' says Ethan, as we part at the end of my road.

'Nothing, I hope,' I say. 'I haven't got over the shock of finding those brushes!'

*

But the thieving doesn't stop, even though everyone is being more vigilant now. The next item to vanish is Jassy's iPhone. She announces its disappearance at break.

'Are you going to report it to the police?' Scarlett asks her.

'No, it's no big deal. I can buy another one any time.'

I suppose that's true. Her parents have got enough money to buy the whole factory that makes the iPhones, if they wanted.

'Who d'you reckon it is?' Ethan whispers to me as we pass in the corridor.

'How do I know? We haven't gathered any real evidence yet. So much for being great detectives!'

At that moment, Kyle runs past on his way out to the school field. Ethan grabs my arm.

'Look,' he whispers.

'What?'

'Kyle's trainers.'

We both stare. He's wearing a brand new pair of trainers.

'There's your proof!' Ethan shouts.

I shrug my shoulders. I'm not so sure he's right even, though it does look suspicious.

'Kyle is definitely our number one suspect,' he says.

'I suppose so,' I say. 'But … you know I said I feel sorry for him because his family is so poor? Well, I've been thinking … being poor doesn't make him a thief.'

'But … ' Ethan frowns. 'Where did he get the money to buy those trainers?'

'Why don't you ask him?'

'OK,' he calls, as he runs after Kyle. 'Don't worry, Grace. I'll soon get a confession out of him.'

By the end of break, we have an answer.

'Kyle wasn't very pleased at being asked,' Ethan tells me. 'Got all aggressive. But when I insisted, he had the perfect explanation. His dad's got a new job at last.'

'Good.' I'm relieved. A warm feeling washes over me, like when the sun comes out from behind a cloud. I can't explain why, but I didn't want Kyle to be the guilty one.

'I don't think we should cross him off the list yet, though,' Ethan argues.

This detective work is turning out to be more complicated than I thought.

Next, someone's necklace is stolen from the girls' changing room.

'We'll have to cross Kyle off now,' I tell Ethan. 'It can't have been him … '

'Unless he sneaked in there, the perv … '

'Which I doubt.'

Then I find out from my mum's friend, Sue, that Megan's previous trouble and the reason for her social worker had nothing to do with thieving. (Sue won't tell me what it was, though, but from the way she shuddered I have the creepy feeling it was about something horrible that was done *to* Megan, more than something she did!)

Besides, Megan hasn't been in school since the Incredible Hulk incident and Ms Joseph's pen has disappeared.

'That cuts out Megan,' I sigh. 'Now we have no suspects. We'll have to start again.'

The next day, Ethan spots Jassy using an iPhone.

'I thought she'd lost it,' he says.

'That's easy,' I explain. 'She's been out and bought a new one.'

'But it looks just like her old one.'

I get closer to Jassy during the next lesson. He's right. I'm sure it has her old pink case on. I recognise the scratch down one side. I decide to ask her about it.

'Jassy,' I say at break. 'I really need to text my mum, but I've left my phone at home. I couldn't borrow yours, could I?'

' 'Course you can.'

She pulls her iPhone out of her bag. I'm positive it is her old one.

'I thought you'd lost this,' I say.

'Oh, yes, Grace,' she answers with a warm smile that melts my doubt like chocolate in the sun. 'I forgot to tell you. It wasn't stolen after all. I found it in the side pocket of my bag.'

I take the iPhone and text some rubbish to Mum, thank Jassy then hurry to find Ethan.

'Definitely fishy!' he says when I tell him.

'Why?'

'Well, why did she make a fuss about losing it, then 'forget' to tell everyone she'd found it. Perhaps she's our thief.'

'Don't be stupid! Why would Jassy want to steal anything? She has everything she wants, you know that!'

'Yeah.' Ethan holds his hands up and grins. 'Just joking!'

We're back to square one. No suspects, but the thief is still at work.

We'll have to be more vigilant if we're going to solve this mystery before Mrs Metcalf calls in the police.

FIVE

On Saturday morning, I head for my clarinet lesson. It's on the other side of town, so I cycle there with my clarinet case in a pack on my back. I always pass Jassy's house on the way, and often imagine what it must be like to live there. When I was in fairy tale mode, I would see a knight in shining armour rescuing a princess from the turret on the corner of the house. More recently, in twenty-first century mode, I'm invited by a famous pop star to swim in the pool that shimmers behind the house in the enormous gardens.

Today, I'm in sci-fi mode as I begin to cycle past, but I'm just imagining aliens landing their craft on the roof when a movement in the driveway snaps me back to the real world. I brake and skid to a stop behind a car parked on the opposite side of the road. A man and a woman have come out of the front door of Jassy's house and are climbing into a smart red open-top sports car in the driveway. The man is dark and good-looking, but the woman's appearance makes me gasp. She's tall and slender, with flowing blonde hair that flickers with iridescent lights as she tosses her head in laughter … the mirror image of Jassy. She must be her mum.

They slam the doors, the engine purrs like a contented cat and they drive away without looking back. Then I look up at the house. Jassy is at the window at the top of the turret, but I hardly recognise her as she watches the car until it disappears round the corner. There is no sign of the radiance that lights up our class. It's as if the candle has been blown out.

She hasn't seen me and turns away from the window. I ride on, but I can't get that sad expression in her eyes out of my mind.

I'm still wondering about it on Monday when I meet Ethan on the bus, so I tell him what I saw. He's as puzzled as I am, especially as, when we arrive in class, Jassy is there, back to her dazzling self.

We're given another lecture by Ms Joseph about the seriousness of the thefts. 'If no one comes forward to own up by the end of this week,' she warns, 'Mrs Metcalf will call in the police. She would prefer not to, as we do not want to tarnish the excellent reputation of the school, but this thieving cannot go on. Do you all understand?'

'Yes, Ms Joseph,' we all mumble.

I feel the heat surging to my face again as a few people turn to look at me. For the first time ever, I am being noticed … but for all the wrong reasons. They haven't forgotten the paintbrushes. Nor have I! I tremble when I remember Ms Joseph's accusing eyes.

'Let me remind you all that Jassy is our class prefect,' says Ms Joseph. 'If you don't feel you can talk to me in the first instance, I hope you will confide in her. All right, Jassy?'

'Oh yes, Ms Joseph, of course.' Jassy beams her brightest smile.

'Right, class, it's time you were heading for your first lesson.'

'I've said it before,' Ethan mutters when we're in the corridor. 'And I'll say it again. There's something fishy about Jassy. She's not all she makes out.'

'You're wrong,' I whisper. 'I like her. Just because she seemed unhappy at the weekend, that doesn't mean she's a thief. She has everything she could ever want … she's lovely … and so popular … Just look at her now.'

Ethan watches Jassy, who is walking confidently in front with her usual entourage of fluttering females. 'Yeah, I suppose you're right,' he says. 'But we still need to find some new suspects from somewhere. And fast!'

I nod. But from where – and who?

SIX

Fingers point. People accuse each other. Scarlett's dad has been into school to complain, but although several more small items vanish, there is still no evidence.

Ethan and I are feeling as deflated as balloons after a party ... that is, until another electric explosion of genius flashes through my brain.

'I've got it!' I shout.

Ethan glances around, but there's no one near. We're walking home across the park.

'What?'

'A way to trap the thief! I'm going to plant a pair of my earrings in the classroom and keep watch.'

Ethan runs his fingers through his hair. 'Great thinking, partner!' he drawls, in an atrocious attempt at an American accent. 'Tomorrow, huh?'

That evening, I find my shiniest bling earrings, a pair I bought in a charity shop for a few pence a while ago. I've never really liked them. I hide them in my bag.

First lesson is in our own form room, so I decide that break is the best time to lay my trap. I'm slow packing my books away after the lesson and Ms Joseph has long click-clacked from the room. Ethan makes a botched attempt at a wink as he leaves.

I'm alone. Quickly, I lift the earrings from my bag and place them in the middle of the desk. No point in concealing them. The thief will want a swift snatch and away. I'm not very big, so I fit quite well underneath a corner table where a cloth hangs halfway to the floor. Then all I have to do is wait.

Five minutes pass, then ten. The bell will be ringing for the end of break shortly and I'll have wasted my time. Then the door slowly opens. I hear light footsteps as someone tiptoes in. I can only see the feet as whoever it is ambles around the room for a few seconds, pounces on my desk like a puma onto its prey, then swivels round and darts from the room.

Peeping out, I recognise the back of a tall elegant figure with blonde hair. It's Jassy!

As soon as the door has closed behind her, I spring from my hidey-hole like a gazelle and leap to my desk. The earrings have gone! Jassy? It can't be true! But my eyes didn't deceive me. There is no denying it.

My whole body is trembling like a dish of jelly as I nod to Ethan next lesson and mouth one word.

'Jassy!'

'I told you she was suspect,' he says at lunchtime. 'It must have been her that planted those paint brushes in your bag.'

'But she stuck up for me, said it couldn't have been me. Why would she do that?'

Ethan frowns. 'Maybe she had a hunch we'd all be searched and your bag was the nearest ... then she felt guilty for landing you in it.'

'Suppose so.'

'And another clue ... when the science stuff went missing, Jassy leapt ten feet into the air when Ms Joseph said her name.'

I nodded. 'Yeah. I noticed that, too.'

'So what do you aim to do now?'

I'd already thought about that. Actually, I'd been

thinking of nothing else since break. My head just wouldn't accept that Jassy could be a thief. There must be some other explanation.

'I've decided there's only one way to find out. I'm going to leave school with her this afternoon and confront her. But you'll have to help.'

'How?'

'Well, she always zips out of school double quick. I can't keep up with her. So you'll have to waylay her somehow.'

'Any ideas?'

'Oh, I don't know … pretend to fall over, something like that.'

I'm as restless as a tree on a windy day. The lessons seem so long and I find it impossible to concentrate on anything, but at last the final bell goes. Ethan is out of the blocks like an Olympic sprinter and leaves the classroom just in front of Jassy. I hear a crash and a yell.

Ethan will need an Oscar for his performance, by the sound of it.

I emerge into the corridor just as Jassy is picking him up off the floor.

'Oh, thanks, Jassy,' he says, carefully avoiding looking at me. 'Silly me. Tripped over me own feet. See you tomorrow.'

He sprints off. As Jassy begins to hurry away, I call her back.

'Jassy, can I walk with you today?' I ask. 'I'm going your way.'

She seems surprised. 'Oh, er, yes, of course, if you like.'

I catch up with her and we leave the building together.

'There's something I wanted to ask you,' I begin, hoping my voice doesn't sound as shaky as I feel.

She looks down at me with cool blue eyes.

'Yes?'

I've always admired Jassy and now I'm about to accuse her of stealing from me. It would be so much easier to chicken out. But I have to do it. I gulp down my nerves.

'I left some earrings on my desk this morning at break. Did you take them?'

SEVEN

Jassy stops and turns to me. 'What are you suggesting?'

'I … '

I know I've turned lobster red, but grip my fists tightly to make myself speak. 'Th … that you're the thief.'

'What?'

Her eyes have widened into blue mountain lakes.

'I ... I left my earrings on my desk today ... as a trap to catch the thief ... and you came into the room and took them. I was hiding. I saw you.'

She laughs like the tinkling of tiny bells. 'Oh Grace!' she sighs. 'Of course I took them. I saw them there on your desk, so I assumed they were yours. I thought you wouldn't want them to be stolen. Then I forgot to give them back to you. Sorry.'

She feels in her pocket and hands them to me. I take them, feeling a mixture of relief, because I've always refused to believe that she is our thief, and disappointment, because it seemed Ethan and I were getting nearer to success.

'Thanks.' It's all I can say.

'See you tomorrow,' she says.

I'm left standing, rooted to the spot. As I watch her walk quickly away, I wonder if she hates me for accusing her, and I almost call her back to apologise. Then my brain goes into overdrive. She was very quick with her excuse for having my earrings. But why did she 'forget' to give them to me, when we went to the same lesson almost immediately after she had taken them? Was she lying?

There's no time to talk to Ethan about this, so I'll have to go it alone. She's an enigma and I want to crack her code. I begin to follow her long-legged stride and am soon quite out of breath. I presume she'll go straight home, but she turns in the opposite direction, towards the town centre. I almost catch her up, then hang back, panting, dodging behind lampposts, rubbish bins and pillar boxes in true detective mode.

She pauses outside a jeweller's shop, so I nip into a dress shop doorway nearby, get my breath back and peer out at her. She's staring in the shop window. She stays there for so long I begin to worry that I'll be told to clear off. I'm in the way of customers going in and out of the shop. I step aside to let them pass.

Jassy's gone! My eyes frantically scour the street, but

she's vanished. I dash to the jeweller's shop. The door is ajar and I peep inside. She's there, standing at a counter, talking in her bright, confident manner to a young man. He's mesmerised by her, as everyone is.

He fetches out a tray of silver necklaces. She fingers them all, smiling up at the young man, talking all the time. He goes to fetch another tray and, as his back is turned, Jassy slips a chain from the edge of the tray into her pocket. I clap my hand over my mouth to stop an audible gasp and force myself to stay calm.

The young man returns, but he is so spellbound by her he is oblivious to the missing necklace. Again, Jassy touches each chain in turn, then she laughs her tinkling bell laugh and shakes her head, so the shop lights glint in her hair.

'Thank you so much,' I hear her say.

Before she turns towards the door, I dart away. Bobbing down behind an advertising board, I see her leave the shop, a satisfied smile on her face. She walks briskly away. What should I do? Rush into the shop to report the crime? Pretend nothing happened and go home? Or follow her? My choice is easy. I set off after her.

There's no doubt in my mind now. Jassy must be the thief! But what makes a beautiful rich kid steal?

This time, she heads for home. Five minutes later, she's arrived at her front door and is putting the key in the lock. Without hesitating, I dash the last few metres.

'Jassy!' I shout.

She whips round, the door half open. 'Grace? What are you doing here?'

'I want to know why,' I say, gasping for breath. 'Why do you do it?'

'Do what?'

'I think you know what I mean, Jassy. I saw you in that jeweller's shop.'

'Have you been spying on me?'

She faces me with hands on her slim hips, fire bursting from ice-cold eyes.

I stare at the ground and nod.

'Well, thank you very much! What's this, a police state?'

'No, Jassy.' I speak quietly, trying to calm things down.

'Just because you're a bit of an oddball, it doesn't mean you can go accusing the rest of us. That's ridiculous!'

'But there've been so many things go missing … '

'So?'

'So Ethan and I … '

'Ethan … that creep?'

'He's OK … He and I have been investigating.'

'Investigating? You fancy yourselves as Holmes and Watson?'

I try to stick to what I need to say. 'I had three suspects … him, Kyle and Megan, but it's not any of them … and I was a suspect for a while, if you remember.'

Her face is so pale it's almost translucent. Suddenly, there is panic in her eyes. 'Who else is in on this?' she whispers.

'No one. I promise. And Ethan doesn't know I followed you today.'

She nods, then steps into her house. I expect the door to be slammed in my face, but she beckons me in.

EIGHT

We enter a palace. Large rooms full of white leather sofas, oil paintings on walls, Egyptian rugs on polished wooden floors. There's nothing out of place and the contrast between this and my family's small, untidy house with my two little brothers roaring through like tornados stuns me. It's like a show home. Jassy leads me up a carpeted staircase that curves towards the top, then along a wide corridor. At last, she stops outside a white door and leads me in. The curved walls tell me immediately that this is the turret I saw her in on Saturday.

'Sit down,' she says, pointing to an enormous bed. I sink into a mattress as soft as marshmallows. She sits opposite me, perched on the edge of an armchair.

'Grace, you've always been so quiet, but I guess you see everything.'

I nod.

'And I bet you're good at keeping secrets?'

'Yes.'

My heart is racing.

'When I took your earrings, I'm afraid what I said wasn't quite truthful.'

I remain silent, holding my breath. I feel she's on the verge of saying something momentous.

'And just now in town … '

'Yes?'

'You won't report me, will you?'

I swallow hard.

'Well,' I murmur. 'That depends.'

She sighs. 'Grace, I can't help it … I'm like a magpie … you know, they're supposed to be attracted to shiny things. That's exactly me. Ever since I was little I've been a bit of collector … but lately … I was hoping you'd understand.'

She suddenly lunges across the room, dives under my feet and reaches under her bed. Pulling out a pink and purple weekend case, she lifts it up and sits beside me on the bed, plonking the case on her lap. Then she unzips the lid.

I think I'm ready for anything, but I draw a sharp

intake of breath which almost chokes me. The case is brimming with loot. I recognise Sandeep's watch straight away, then metal tongs from the science lab and Edward's cricket ball.

'Why?' I ask again. 'You've got a home to die for, you're rich, you can have everything you want … '

'Except what I want most in the world.'

I turn sharply to look at her. Tears are streaming down her face. I want to hug her and make it better, but I don't understand what can possibly be missing in her life.

'What's that?' I ask.

'Parents who love me.'

My mind takes a rollercoaster ride. I'd never have guessed that in a million years.

'But surely they love you … '

'No, they don't,' she cries. 'They didn't want any children. Then I came along. So they merely tolerate me. Mum spends most of her time abroad with her super-high-flyer job and Dad is out at his club or on the golf course when he's not at work. I've had au pair after au pair after au pair, and now I'm too old for that I'm so lonely.'

'But you're the most popular person in class!' I protest. 'I'm the one that no one notices.'

I put my arm around her shoulders and let her sob while I try to think what to say … what to do.

'Please don't rat on me.'

I'm in a quandary. I know she trusts me enough to show me this, but how can I keep it to myself? She's a master thief. If I don't split on her it makes me almost as guilty. My brain churns rapidly, trying to work out a solution. Then, as usual, a surge of electricity crashes through my head with an idea.

'I won't rat,' I say. 'But on one condition.'

NINE

Next morning, I ride on the bus with Ethan.

'I've cracked it!' I whisper.

A giant question mark of a frown appears on his forehead. 'On your own?'

'Yeah.' His eyes show me he feels hurt.

'Sorry,' I say. 'It all happened rather quickly.'

'So who … ?'

'I've promised I won't say a word, but I'll tell you later.'

He frowns. 'Grace?'

'Sorry,' I say again.

In class, Jassy's brilliance shines as usual, as if our conversation and her confession had never occurred, but no one except me notices her for once. All eyes are on Sandeep, who suddenly discovers his watch under a pile of books on his desk. Ms Joseph smiles as she writes with her missing pen and Sally's pencil case miraculously turns up in her bag.

At break, Scarlett shrieks loudly enough to deafen the whole school. She has found her ring on the floor of the cloakroom. Edward's cricket ball rolls mysteriously towards him across the field. In science, Mrs Davey rejoices in the reappearance of her missing equipment.

The class sounds like a murder of gossiping crows. Nobody can understand how everything that was stolen has now so unexpectedly turned up.

'You must be a magician,' Ethan says to me. 'So, are you going to let me into the secret yet?'

'Later ... sorry.'

I feel bad that I'm keeping him in the dark, but a promise is a promise, and Jassy is keeping her side of the bargain.

At lunchtime, she and I sneak out of school and hurry to the centre of town. I feel her tension like red hot wires between us, but she doesn't flinch as we enter the jeweller's and head for the same young man. His eyes reflect her glow as she approaches.

'I'm really sorry,' she begins in a voice that sounds far away. 'But when I was in here yesterday ... '

'I remember,' says the young man. 'You were looking at our silver chains ... '

'When I got home … ' Jassy's face has that translucent look again. She feels for my hand and I grip hers firmly. ' … I found that one of your chains had slipped off the tray into my bag.'

She holds out the chain.

He frowns. 'But … '

'I'm so sorry.' Jassy puts her head on one side. 'Perhaps it wasn't fastened securely.'

That seems to persuade him. He smiles back. 'Thank you for being so honest,' he says, as he takes it from her. I hear her swallow hard and we turn and walk out of the shop.

'Phew!' she says as we head back towards school. 'That was the hardest thing I've ever had to do, but I feel so good that I managed it … thanks to you, Grace.'

I smile. 'Now we must enter the volcano and meet the fire-eating monster.'

My knees tremble like butterfly wings as we knock on Mrs Metcalf's door a few minutes later, but I squeeze Jassy's shaky hand and she grimaces at me.

'Come!'

Ten minutes later, we are unsinged and alive.

Jassy has told Mrs Metcalf everything and, believe it or not, the headteacher wasn't as fiery or as monstrous as we dreaded. She won't be calling the police, but will make an appointment to talk to Jassy's parents.

'So?' demands Ethan, when he catches me alone. 'I've been driven mad by curiosity all day. Tell!'

So I do.

*

Jassy knows I'll reveal the whole story to Ethan. That was part of the deal to help her out of this mess.

But the most difficult part for her is still to come. I'm going round to her house this evening to support her when she confesses to her parents. I hope she's brave enough to let them know the cause and I hope they will realise that all the money in the world hasn't bought happiness for Jassy. I'm sure, deep down, they must love her really.

For me, some good has come out of all this. I'm no longer boring old Grace, alone and unnoticed. The quiet brown mouse has morphed into somebody much more confident. Ethan and I get along very well and I know that, from now on, Jassy and I are going to be really good friends.

Jill Atkins began her working life as a Primary school teacher, but eventually escaped and ran a Bed & Breakfast for several years. This is when she began writing in earnest. She's had over 60 books published with a variety of publishers.

Jill lives with her husband in West Sussex and loves spending time with her children and five grandchildren.